Wilma Jean the Worry Machine

Activity and Idea Book

published by

NATIONAL CENTER for YOUTH ISSUES

A Note to Parents and Educators:

Anxiety is a subjective sense of worry, apprehension, and/or fear. It is considered to be the number one health problem in America. Although quite common, anxiety disorders in children are often misdiagnosed or overlooked. It is normal for everyone to feel fear, worry, and apprehension from time to time, but when these feelings prevent a person from doing what he/she wants and/or needs to do, anxiety becomes a disability.

The purpose of this book is to offer creative activities for counselors, teachers, and parents that can lessen the severity of anxiety in children. The ultimate goal is to provide children with the tools they need to feel in control of their anxiety.

I hope you enjoy doing these activities as much as I have enjoyed creating them. Now, take a deep breath, and let the fun begin!!!

BEST!

Julia Cook

Duplication and Copyright

NATIONAL CENTER for
YOUTH ISSUES

P.O. Box 22185
Chattanooga, TN 37422-2185
423.899.5714 • 866.318.6294
fax: 423.899.4547
www.ncyi.org

ISBN: 978-1-937870-03-4 $9.95
© 2012 National Center for Youth Issues, Chattanooga, TN
All rights reserved.

Summary: A supplementary teacher's guide for *Wilma Jean the Worry Machine*.
Full of discussion questions and exercises to share with students.

Written by: Julia Cook
Contributing Editor: Laurel Klaassen
Illustrations by: Anita DuFalla
Published by National Center for Youth Issues

Printed at Starkey Printing
Chattanooga, TN, USA
June 2016

Helpful Tips for Supporting an Anxious Child

- Genuinely accept your child's concerns.

- Listen to your child's perceptions and gently correct misinformation.

- Patiently encourage your child to approach a feared situation one step at a time until it becomes familiar and manageable.

- Always try to get your child to events on time, or early – being late can elevate levels of anxiety.

- Continually set equal expectations for all kids, anxious or not. Expecting a child to be anxious will only encourage anxiety.

- Role-play strategies – give them ideas for how to react in certain situations. Explore both best case scenarios and worst case scenarios using realistic evidence.

- Build your child's personal strengths.

- Help your child organize the next day's school materials the night before.

- Allow and encourage your child to do things on his/her own.

- Allow extra time on tests and/or allow students to take tests away from other students.

- If a child is going to be singled out for a classroom activity, let that child know a day in advance so they can feel more prepared.

- Designate a "safe person" at school that understands your child's worries and concerns.

- Try not to pass your own fears onto your child.

- Work together as a team (family members, teachers, child, day-care providers, etc.).

- Set consequences – don't confuse anxiety with other types of inappropriate behavior. Set limits and consequences so that you don't allow anxiety to enable your child.

- Have reasonable expectations.

The Amazing Worry Doll

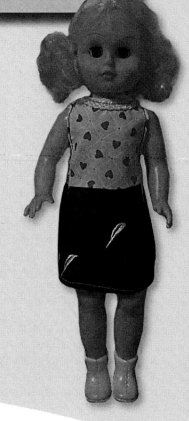

Materials
Small plastic doll for each anxious child – may be new or used. (Easy to find at hobby or craft stores.)

Directions

Your worry doll is AMAZING! You can tell her/him anything! Hold your worry doll in your hand and just start talking. Tell your doll everything you are worried about. As soon as you tell your doll a worry, you have given that worry away to the doll and she/he will hold it for you until you need it back. YES, your doll will worry for you so that you can be worry free!!!

• If you worry at night, tell your doll your worries before you go to bed. Then tuck the doll under your pillow and enjoy a good night's sleep!

• If you worry at school, tell your doll your worries. Then put the doll inside your coat pocket or inside your desk and enjoy a worry free day!

• Your worry doll will work any time and in any place!

If you ever want or need your worries back, just hold your doll in your hand, close your eyes, and let your worries transfer back into your head – but who would want that?!

Square Breathing

Materials
• Paper
• Pen or pencil.

Sometimes, when we feel anxious, we start to breathe too fast. This activity will help you slow down your breathing and help you to relax.

Directions

Draw a clockwise square as you breathe in and out. Start in the left hand bottom corner of your paper. Inhale slowly as you draw a line up. Hold your breath as you slowly draw a line across to the right. Exhale slowly as you draw a line down toward the bottom of the paper. Pause your breathing as you draw a line to the left completing the square. The bigger your square, the slower you breathe.

Try it on paper a few times and then do it in your head without paper. If you want, you can draw your square in the air with your finger as you breathe.

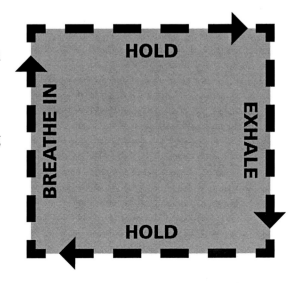

What Are You Worried About?

Directions

In the space below, make a list of <u>everything</u> you are worried about.
Use the back of this paper if you need more room.

_____   _____
_____   _____
_____   _____
_____   _____
_____   _____
_____   _____

Now rewrite your list of worries and put them in order from your biggest worry to your smallest worry (use the back if you need more room.)

BIGGEST

1. _____   6. _____
2. _____   7. _____
3. _____   8. _____
4. _____   9. _____
5. _____   10. _____

SMALLEST

1. _____   6. _____
2. _____   7. _____
3. _____   8. _____
4. _____   9. _____
5. _____   10. _____

Can You Control Your Worries?

Use your list of worries from page 5 and write them where you think they belong on the chart below.

Worries I Can Control

Worries I Can't Control

Brainstorm ideas and solutions for moving your worries up to the "**Worries I Can Control**" part of your paper. For the worries that are not in your control, try using a worry doll or a worry hat so you can feel worry-free more of the time.

I Feel It "Here"!

Directions

When we worry, we can feel it anywhere!

1. Take turns tracing each other on the bulletin board paper. You can pose any way you want to!

2. Cut out the figure of yourself and draw your face on your figure.

When you worry about something, where can you feel it?

3. Draw what worry feels like or write the word "worry" on your body every place that you feel it when you are worried about something.

4. Compare your body cut-out to others. Does worrying affect other people the same way it affects you?

A Chain of Events: Thoughts to Feelings

Materials
- Strips of lightly colored construction paper cut 1 1/2" X 12"
- Pen or Pencil
- Glue Stick or Stapler

What we are thinking can directly lead to how we are feeling, both in good and bad situations.

Directions

1. Think of something that happened that made you feel worried or anxious. Write down what happened on one of the strips of paper. Glue or staple that strip into a circle.

2. Write down what you thought (worst case scenario) when this happened to you on another strip of paper. Attach that strip to the first one like a paper chain.

3. Write down how you felt on another strip of paper and attach that strip to the first two strips.

4. Look at your three-link chain. Can you see how what you think about a situation dictates how you will feel about it?

Now Try Again

1. Think of something that happened that made you feel worried or anxious. Write down what happened on one of the strips of paper. Glue or staple that strip into a circle.

2. Write down what you thought (best case scenario – using only positive thoughts.) Attach that strip to the first one like a paper chain.

3. Write down how your more positive thoughts made you feel on another strip of paper and attach that strip to the first two.

4. Look at your three-link chain. Can you see how what you think about a situation can dictate how you will feel about it?

How Do You Feel?

*"By the time I got to school,
I felt like I'd swallowed an elephant
playing the banjo!"*

This is how Wilma Jean felt when
she was anxious about school.

Complete the following sentence about a time when you felt anxious or worried.
Then, in the space below, draw a picture of what the inside of your stomach felt like.

"By the time I got to _____ I felt like

I'd swallowed a _____."

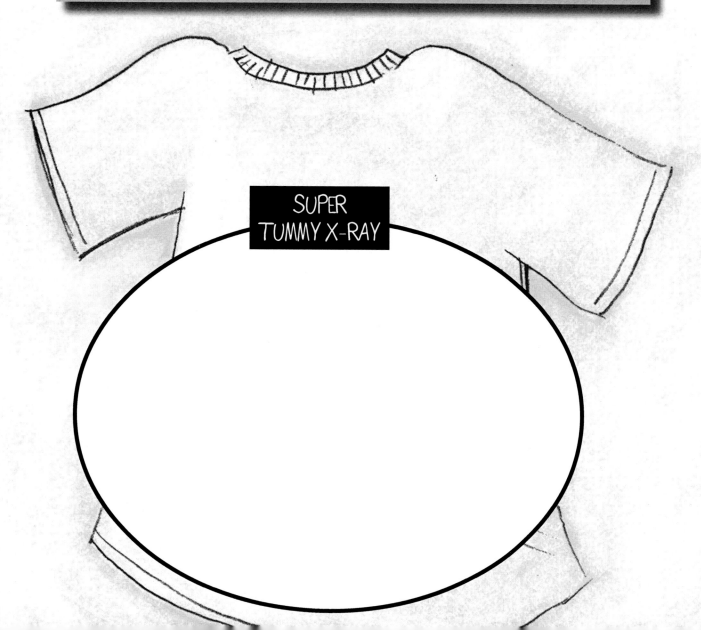

SUPER
TUMMY X-RAY

The Worry Button

Sometimes we worry when someone we love is not nearby. For example, you may miss your mom while you are at school or your dad while he is at work, etc.

Materials
- A random collection of several buttons – all shapes, types, colors, etc.
- Yarn or string

Directions

1. Spread all of the buttons out on a flat surface.
2. Look at them carefully and choose one that best reminds you of the person that you are worried about.
3. Make a necklace out of the button using string or yarn.
4. Whenever you start to worry, and you need to feel close to your special person, squeeze the button between your fingers and think happy thoughts. Squeeze all your worries away.

The Root Beer Worry Float

Materials
- Vanilla Ice Cream
- One Tall Drinking Glass Per Person
- Root beer
- Spoons
- Napkins

Directions

Compare worrying to making a root beer float as explained below:

- Worrying is like a root beer float. The ice cream represents all that we have going on in our lives, and the root beer represents worrying. Worrying a little bit can be a good thing. (Pour just the right amount of root beer into the glass of ice cream and explain how everyone worries and worrying a little bit is ok).

- When we worry too much, our lives get messy (Pour too much root beer into the glass and watch it overflow). This causes us to over-react and makes a mess out of the stuff we have going on in our lives.

- Expand on this visualization using personal experiences.

- Clean up your mess and let kids make their own root beer floats using just the right amount of "worry." Enjoy!

The Worry Monster

Materials
- An empty tissue box
- Construction paper
- Markers
- Scissors
- Glue

Directions

Decorate the empty tissue box to resemble the head of a cute looking monster. Make the opening of the box a mouth by gluing teeth around the edges.

This is our worry monster. He will help eat our worries away.

Have children write down what they are worried about on small strips of paper. Have them feed the worry monster by placing their worries into his mouth.

Frequently check and remove the worry strips, monitoring each worry situation individually. Intervene when needed.

Explain that time cures a lot of worries. Revisit some of the worries with your class as a group in a generic way. (I was worried about my spelling test, but now that worry is gone because my test is over, etc.).

Worry Rocks

Materials

- Rocks in various sizes - ranging from the size of a tangerine to a small pebble. (These can be collected outside or purchased in a craft store).
- Small disposable plastic cup – one per child
- Water
- Strips of paper
- Pencil or pen

This is a visual activity to help children understand that we only have room in our lives for a limited amount of worries, and if we worry too much about the little things, we won't be able to handle the big things.

Directions:

1. Using the strips of paper, have children write down all of the things they are worrying about.

2. Have children separate rocks into three piles by size. (Small, Medium, and Large)

3. Have children divide up their worry strips into three categories similar to the rock piles. (Small Worries, Medium Sized Worries, and Large Worries).

4. Fill the cups half full with water. The water represents all of the stuff they have going on in their lives, and the rocks represent their worries.

5. For each worry, have children drop the right sized rock into their cup. If their cup flows over, they have too many worries. Have them re-examine their worry strips and work on removing some of them through logical thought and realistic evidence. They may also end up needing to remove worries over which they do not have control.

6. Children will see first-hand that if you have too many small worries in your life, you won't have room to deal with your bigger worries.

From Trash to Treasure to Trash!

Materials
- One plastic grocery bag per student
- One pair of latex gloves per student
- Litter found inside of the school building
- Poster boards
- Markers
- Glue

Teacher Instructions

Have students spread out throughout the building and pick up litter, paper scraps, and trash found in the halls and on floors of the classrooms.

Using the litter that has been collected, have each student create a worry poster. Each item on the poster can symbolize something they are worried about or how they feel when they are worried.

When the posters are completed, have each student explain his/her poster to the rest of the class.

Discuss with the class how recognizing our worries can help us overcome them. Also, by collecting litter and cleaning up the school, our school has become an even better place.

Keep the worry posters on display for one day.

As a class, rip up the posters to symbolize "ripping up" and "being in control of" your worries. Throw the ripped posters into the trash and "DISPOSE" of both the posters AND your worries.

Now, not only did you rid the school of litter, you made your mind a better place by disposing of the worries that were polluting your thoughts.

My First Worry

Instructions

Think back to the very first time you remember worrying about something.

Who/what were you worried about?

_____

Why were you worried?

_____

What did you do to show that you were worried?

_____

Did anyone else notice you were worried?

_____

Draw a picture of your first memory of being worried.

My Last Worry

Think about the last time you felt worried about something.

Who/what were you worried about?

_____

Why were you worried?

_____

What did you do to show that you were worried?

_____

Did anyone else notice that you were worried?

_____

Draw a picture of the last time you felt worried.

Has your worrying gotten better or worse over time? Explain.

_____

_____

Worry, Worry Snowball Fight

Materials
- 8 1/2" x 11" sheets of plain white paper (two per person)
- Pencils

Instructions

Worrying can make you uptight. Here is a great way to unwind!

- Pass out two sheets of paper to each student and to the teacher.

- Have everyone in the class (teacher included) fill both sheets by writing down all of their worries. (for example, "I am worried about my spelling test next week." Or "I am worried that my parents might be getting a divorce.")

- Have students and teacher wad up their papers into tight balls.

- Have a "snowball fight" for three to five minutes.

- At the end of the snowball fight, collect all of the worry snowballs, put them into a paper or plastic sack, and throw them away in the trash. Be careful not to reveal what is on the snowball papers, as some worries are private.

- Say: "After what you just put your worries through, they will be in no shape to bother you again for awhile."

Teachers: You may want to read through the worry snowball papers privately, if concerned.

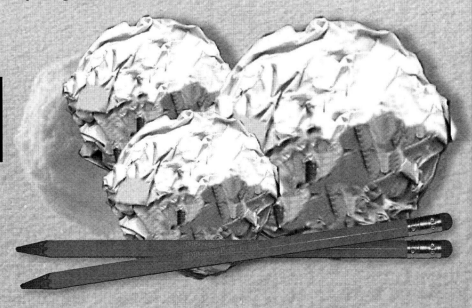

16

Worry Beans

Materials
- Large tub
- Many bags of beans – different colors and sizes

Directions

Fill tub ¾ of the way full of dried beans. Mix up beans.

When kids feel stressed or anxious, let them "play in the beans." Have them run their fingers and hands through the beans and use this feeling to help them breathe and relax.

If you as a teacher believe in the "soothing powers" of the beans, so will your students. Soft background music helps, too!

The Worry Hat

Materials
One hat – Any shape or color, but big enough to fit anyone's head

Sometimes we worry about things over which we have no control (the weather, parents are getting divorced, teacher being absent, dad lost his job, etc.)

When this happens, and your uncontrollable worries take over, break out the Worry Hat!

Put on the worry hat, close your eyes, and "think" all of your worries you cannot control into the hat. Turn the hat upside down and it will hold your worries for you.

If you ever want, or need, them back, you can put on the hat, close your eyes again, and "think" them back into your head.

Magic Worry Milk

The purpose of this activity is to create a visual for how anxiety and worry can make you feel on the inside.

Materials

- One 9"x 13" clear glass baking pan
- Whole milk
- Food coloring
- Liquid dish soap

Directions:

- Pour enough milk in the pan to cover the bottom (1/4" to 1/2" deep) – *This represents you as a person.*

- Using the food coloring, create any design you want. *– Each color stands for something in your life that is going on or something you need to do. When all is still, you can handle everything!*

- Aim the liquid dish soap at the center of the pan and allow two or three drops of dish soap to fall into the milk. *This represents the anxiety you have.*

- Do not stir.

- Watch as the milk starts to swirl and the colors start to travel and mix. The soap churns the milk and the colors start to move and mix together until eventually, they become unrecognizable. *This represents what anxiety does to you. Anxiety churns you up inside and mixes everything up – making it harder for you to recognize what is going on in your life and what you need to get done.*

- When you can control your anxiety, you can stop the soap from getting into the milk and you can learn to handle everything more effectively.

Worry-Free T-Shirt

Materials

- T-shirt diagram below
- Markers and/or colored pencils
- Plain white T-shirt (can be new or used)
- Fabric markers and/or paints

Directions

- You work for a design company and it is your job to create a "Worry-Free T-Shirt." Whenever a person wears the shirt, all of his/her worries disappear.

- Practice creating your design using the T-shirt diagram below. Then, decorate your T-shirt with the fabric paint and let dry overnight.

- Wear your creation with pride and enjoy having a "Worry-Free" day!

Worry or Unworry? Which Side am I on?

Materials
- Stack of 3" x 5" index cards
- Pen or pencil
- Piece of paper

Directions

- List every worry you have, no matter how big or how small, on the piece of paper.

- Fold your index cards in half vertically (See Figure A).

- Write down one worry on the left side of each index card until you have used all of the cards needed.

- Take one of your worry cards and think of an unworry or two you can write on the right side of your card. Explain what you can do to make the worry go away. (See Examples below).

EXAMPLES

Worry	Unworry
I am worried about my math test.	I will study for it every night this week. I will ask my teacher for practice problems to help me get ready. I will ask my big sister or my mom to show me how to do the hard problems. I will come prepared.
I think my parents might get divorced.	I did not cause this, I cannot control this, so I have to learn to cope with it. I can only worry about the things I can control. I can be in control of my school work and how I choose to act.
We might have a tornado.	I cannot control the weather. I have a tornado safety plan in place. The logical chances of having a tornado today are very slim. It doesn't make sense for me to hang on to this worry.

FIGURE A

Words of Worry

Find the words in the puzzle. Look horizontal, vertical, and diagonal.
All words are right-reading. Answer key is below.

```
W O R R Y E A S S M I L E P S
C D Y M C I S R C D P P L Q M
A E B A A B T G O N Q O Z N Q
R M F P T C Y R O S R D Y F S
R U D A B K H E K T C E E E B
O H P N P R G I N E Y S D G M
T N R T W I E O N I A A U C R
S T W P I E C A S E R N A S E
F L U R U G J K T G I X V W L
C P S E I E H Y L H M J N E A
B Q X D B Q W T D E E I O A X
T A P I O C A C H A N G E T L
B N L C B U T T E R E D Z H W
C O F T C O N F I D E N C E G
J A N X I E T Y K Z I B C R T
```

Worry	Confidence
Machine	Change
Anxiety	Grades
Uptight	Weather
Relax	Pickle
Breathe	Face
Smile	Cook
Flu	Tapioca
Tease	Buttered
Control	Carrots
Predict	

21

What Are They Worried About?

Materials
- Magazines
- Poster boards
- Glue
- Markers or pens

• Look through magazines and cut out faces of people who look worried or anxious. Glue the faces to the poster board. Below each picture, write a caption telling what the person is worried about and why.

• Choose your favorite face and caption, and creatively write a story about your picture below. Include answers to the following questions in your story:

1. Why is the person worried?
2. Is there anything the person can do about the worry? Is this a worry they can control?
3. What is the person planning to do about the worry?
4. What can the person do to help control how much he/she worries?
5. Are you like the person in your story?
6. What do you do to control your worries?

Worry-Free Escape Bottle

Watching flowing liquids, or other materials, over time (i.e. sand passing through an hour glass) can have a calming effect as it serves as a mental escape. Items such as lava lamps, glitter sticks, and oil and water jars are perfect…or, you can make your own!

Materials
- One 20 oz. empty water bottle or clear soda bottle with the label removed
- One cup hot water
- One tablespoon Glitter Glue
- Additional glitter (different or same color)
- Two tablespoons cooling oil (optional)

Directions
1. Pour hot water into bottle.
2. Add glitter glue.
3. Add additional glitter.
4. Screw on lid tightly.
5. Shake, watch, and escape!

For an even different effect, add cooking oil to bottle.

Wilma Jean's Bad Hair Day

**Wilma Jean worries about her hair.
She tries to fix it, but it goes EVERYWHERE!**

Directions

Give the "Wilma Jean" below bad hair.
Make it as crazy as you can.

When the hair stylist came to Wilma Jean's class, she taught everybody how to do a better job on their hair. Now give Wilma Jean a great hair style.

Directions

You just woke up with the worst hair ever! You only have 10 minutes to eat and get to school. Using the figure below, draw a picture of yourself having a really, really bad hair day.

Then, draw a picture of yourself with great hair!

"Stick It" To Your Worries!

Directions

1. Brainstorm as many strategies as you can that will help you control your worries. Your strategies can be for you or for someone else. Write every strategy on your paper.

2. Write each strategy on a craft stick.

3. Place all of the craft sticks in a jar.

4. Now, whenever you feel worried or anxious, "stick it" to your worry by pulling a stick from the jar and doing what it tells you to do.

Note: If the first stick you pull doesn't work for your worry, pull another stick. Keep pulling until you find one that works!

Strategies can include:

• Talk to someone who will really listen to what you have to say.

• Approach a feared situation one step at a time until it becomes familiar and manageable.

• Picture yourself doing great, wonderful things. Close your eyes and see it in your head!

• Always plan to be on time or early.

• Do everything you can to prepare for your event.

• Don't expect yourself to be anxious. Tell yourself that you will be fine.

• Role-play strategies – how to react in certain situations.

• Concentrate on your personal strengths. Think of something you do really well.

• Organize your school materials for the next day on the night before.

• Try harder to do things on your own.

• Ask your teacher to allow you a little extra time on tests and/or allow you to take tests away from other students.

• Ask your teacher to let you know a day in advance if you are going to be singled out for a classroom activity.

• Designate a "safe person" at school who understands you. When you need to, go talk to that person.

• Don't let other people's fears become yours.

• Work together as a team (family members, teachers, child, day-care providers, etc.).

• Don't use your anxiety as an excuse to get out of things you are able to do.

• Walk away from your situation and take a "mental vacation" for a few minutes.

• Have reasonable expectations about yourself.